UNICORNS

Believe in Magic

summersdale

Summersdale Publishers Ltd
46 West Street
Chichester
West Sussex
PO19 1RP
UK

www.summersdale.com

Printed and bound in the Czech Republic

ISBN: 978-1-84953-956-2

Substantial discounts on bulk quantities of Summersdale books are available to corporations, professional associations and other organisations. For details contact general enquiries: telephone: +44 (0) 1243 771107, fax: +44 (0) 1243 786300 or email: enquiries@summersdale.com

Unicorns...

You probably know some people who don't believe our sparkly friends exist, but then these are probably the same people who don't believe in good luck, true love and happy-ever afters. Don't listen to them! Instead, take a magical trip through the pages of this book and enjoy living in the cute yet kick-ass world of unicorns, where every journey ends with a rainbow and every dream just might come true!

I want
to be a
unicorn.

My other horse is
a unicorn.

Badass unicorn.

UNICORN SELFIE.

In unicorn we trust.

Unicorns don't grow
on trees. They grow on
magic mountains!

KEEP CALM
AND
BE A UNICORN.

Dreams are the playgrounds of unicorns.

What's better than a unicorn?

A SUPERHERO UNICORN!

I feel as happy
as a unicorn
eating cake on
a rainbow.

A unicorn is someone who knows they're MAGICAL and isn't afraid to show it.

YOU EITHER BELIEVE IN
UNICORNS
OR YOU'RE WRONG.

Unicorns are awesome.
I am awesome.
Therefore, I am
a unicorn.

The important thing is that
I believe in myself.

LET'S JUST ALL BE UNICORNS.

Love is... rainbows and unicorns.

"Unicorns are lame,"
said nobody ever.

My head is full of glitter and unicorns.

Always be yourself.

Unless you can be a unicorn.
Then always be a unicorn.

Always be yourself

UNICORN:
a combination of dreams, stardust and sunbeams!

Be like a unicorn: chase rainbows.

SORRY I'M LATE – I SAW A UNICORN.

A friend
told me I was
delusional.
I almost fell off
my unicorn.

Only awesome people...

... can see unicorns.

You were not born
to be perfect.
You were born
to be a unicorn.

MY UNICORN
MADE ME DO IT.

Reaching peak unicorn.

U is for unicorn.

Can't stop –
I moustache.

Everything is better
with a unicorn.

YOU SPARKLE!

I'd rather...

... be a unicorn.

Unicorns will help you reach doughnuts in high places.

You're like a unicorn that brings me ice cream on a sunny day: too good to be true.

You're as sweet as a unicorn fart.

Have ♥ a magical day.

Unicorns
have great hair
but they'll always say
yours looks better.

I'M NOT WEIRD
— I'M A UNICORN.

Unicorns rock.

Being a unicorn
isn't about being real,
it's about being real
AWESOME.

Unleash your inner unicorn!

I POOP

RAINBOWS.

What's inside a unicorn?

Take me home –

I'm yours!

Who says
unicorns
aren't real?

If you're interested in finding out more about our books,
find us on Facebook at *Summersdale Publishers* and
follow us on Twitter at *@Summersdale*.

www.summersdale.com